FOOTBALL

STRUGGLE

Emma Carlson Berne

Raintree is an imprint of Capstone Global Library Limited, a company incorporated in
England and Wales having its registered office at 264 Banbury Road, Oxford, OX2 7DY –
Registered company number: 6695582

www.raintree.co.uk
myorders@raintree.co.uk

Designed by Tracy McCabe
Picture research by Tracy Cummins
Originated by Capstone Global Library Ltd
Printed and bound in India

ISBN 978 1 4747 7136 8
23 22 21 20 19
10 9 8 7 6 5 4 3 2 1

British Library Cataloguing in Publication Data
A full catalogue record for this book is available from the British Library.

Acknowledgements
We would like to thank the following for permission to reproduce photographs:
Shutterstock: rawf8, Design Element, Rob Marmion, Cover.

CONTENTS

CHAPTER 1

TEMPER TROUBLES

A trickle of sweat ran down the side of Liv's face. She stopped the ball with a quick tap of her foot and spun around the Forest Park player. But the defender was closing in.

So Liv snapped the ball to her teammate Samin. The other Falcons player took it and dribbled down the touchline.

Get it to the goal! Liv thought as she ran forward.

But Samin panicked. Two defenders were charging her. She made a sloppy pass to Gabrielle.

Forest Park easily stole the ball. One of their players booted it to the opposite side of the pitch.

Liv let out a frustrated sigh as the other team took the ball closer to the Falcons' goal. The Forest Park striker moved in. She fired off a powerful shot.

Ana, a Falcons defender, leapt just in time to block it. The ball bounced off her shin pad and rolled past the goal line.

The ref blew the whistle and pointed towards the end of the pitch. "Corner kick!" he called. A Forest Park player jogged forward to take it.

Liv bent down and wiped her face with the hem of her top. The score was 4–1 to Forest Park. *We're playing like a bunch of dirty socks,* Liv thought. She felt anger rise up in her and tried to shove it down.

She glanced around at her team, the Falcons. They'd lost their last three matches. This one was on its way to being number four. It was the middle of the second half, and they weren't playing well.

Liv clenched her teeth as she watched the Forest Park player set up the ball. Now Forest Park had *another* good scoring opportunity. Liv could see Coach Davis standing at the edge of the pitch. His clipboard was clasped to his chest. His round, red face looked as stressed as she felt.

Liv's best friend, Dallas, jogged past as she got into place to defend against the corner kick. She rolled her eyes. "Seriously," Dallas mumbled. "Is that girl ever going to take the kick? I could order pizza, take a nap and be back before she's finished setting up."

Liv couldn't help grinning, but she quickly turned her attention back to the Forest Park player. The ref nodded, and the girl backed up from the ball and paused. Then she ran forward and booted it. The game was back on.

The ball soared over to a Forest Park player. She stopped it with a chest bump and tried for a quick shot on goal.

But Rose, playing in defence, snatched it away before the other girl could pull back her leg. Shouts went up from the Falcons as Rose turned the ball. She passed to Rija in midfield.

"Nice, Rose!" Coach shouted.

Rija dribbled right. The other team's winger was all over her. She shot to Dallas at the centre. Dallas kicked to Liv on the left.

The ball thumped against Liv's boot. *OK. Time to get us back in the game,* she thought.

Liv pumped her arms and legs, tapping the ball forward on her laces. Out of the corner of her eye, she could see a Forest Park defender running towards her. Liv zigzagged as she sprinted ahead.

Near the net, Chen was open. Liv got ready to pass to her teammate.

But something suddenly smashed into her legs. Liv tumbled to the ground.

"*Ugh!*" Liv grunted. She pushed herself up and

looked over her shoulder. A Forest Park defender had slid into her from behind. Even with shin pads, Liv could feel prickles of pain on her leg from the other player's studs.

The ball rolled away, and another Forest Park defender grabbed it. She sent it back to her teammates. The ref didn't blow his whistle.

Liv looked around in disbelief as play continued. "Really, ref? That was a foul!"

But the referee just gave Liv a brief glance and a shake of his head.

The girl who had slid into Liv got to her feet. She reached out a hand to help up Liv.

"Seriously?" Liv hissed. Her chest felt tight with anger. She pushed the girl's hand away and stood up on her own.

Ignoring the dull pain in her leg, Liv jogged forward. She just focused on the ball and the pitch.

Dallas had won the ball back. She kicked

to Samin, who easily spun around her defender. Samin brought the ball further down the pitch. In the stands, the onlookers cheered.

Liv ran closer to the goal. Forest Park had left it wide open. They could still turn things around.

"Samin, here!" Liv shouted.

A Forest Park defender was back on Samin. The other player stuck her foot forward, trying to kick the ball out. Samin stumbled to get clear. She made a quick, blind pass.

Liv lurched for the ball – too late. It spun past her boot and shot over the goal line.

"Goal kick!" the ref yelled. He pointed his hand at the Forest Park goal.

"What were you *thinking*, Samin?" The words seemed to burst out of Liv. She couldn't have held them back if she'd tried.

Samin blinked and took a step back. "Sorry!" she said, holding up her hands.

"*Grr!*" Liv stormed off near the touchline.

She aimed a hard kick at an extra ball lying there.

It flew through the air – and smacked Dallas right in the stomach. Her friend fell to the ground.

"Oh no, Dallas! I'm so sorry!" Liv cried. She rushed over. On the way she almost crashed into Coach Davis, who was running forward too. Dallas sat on the grass and clutched her stomach.

"I'm OK," Dallas gasped. "Just got . . . the wind knocked out of me."

Coach helped her up. "Take a minute, Dallas. Go and get some water."

"Dallas–" Liv started to say, but her friend had already turned her back and was walking slowly off the pitch.

"Unsporting behaviour!" the ref called out. "Yellow card, number nine!"

Liv's heart sank. That was her. "Ref, listen–" she began. But his hard eyes looked straight through her.

"Coach?" she pleaded. "Come on!"

"Get on the bench, Liv," Coach said. The coldness in his voice startled her.

Liv looked around. Gabrielle, Nevy and Rija stood grouped near the centre circle. They were staring at her, and they looked angry. Her other teammates were also watching. On the bench, Dallas kept her face turned away.

Liv felt sweat break out on her upper lip. *They're all against me,* she thought wildly. Even the parents in the stands were quiet and staring.

The terrible anger rose up in Liv again. "Fine!" she shouted at Coach.

His face hardened, and he shook his head. Liv clenched her fists and walked stiffly off the pitch. She wanted to scream until she was hoarse.

CHAPTER 2

AWFUL APOLOGIES

Dallas was staring down at her maths textbook when Liv slid into the seat beside her the next morning. Liv dug out her own textbook. She thumped it onto the desk as people rustled into place around her.

"Did you finish the problem set?" Liv asked.

Liv had barely managed to scribble a few answers before flopping into bed last night. After the Forest Park game, she had been too tired and too angry to think about maths.

She was glad her dad was working the evening shift all this week at the auto shop. He hadn't been able to come to the game or ask questions about it afterwards. She didn't want to tell him that she'd got into trouble – again.

Dallas didn't answer. She turned her head away. Her black hair was pulled into a sleek ponytail today.

"Dallas. Dallas!" Liv said again, waving her hand. "Hello!"

She didn't turn around. Liv sighed. "OK, look, I know you're still angry about yesterday. I'm sorry. There. Will you speak to me now?"

Dallas looked back down at her books. Her chin trembled.

Anger rose up in Liv. "Fine! Be that way," she said. She started searching for a pencil.

"I am *not* the problem, Liv Sutcliffe!" Dallas said suddenly.

Liv twisted around. Dallas was staring right at her now. Her brown eyes looked furious.

"I didn't say you were . . . ," Liv said carefully.

"Yes, you did!" Dallas' hands were gripping the edges of her desk. On the other side of her, Kate Patterson looked over curiously. "You always do this, Liv! You lose your temper, you hurt people and then you act like it's no big deal. And if the person doesn't accept your apology – and it's usually an awful apology, by the way – you act like *they* are the ones with the problem. But you have the problem here. Not me!"

Dallas folded her arms on her chest and turned away.

Liv's face was flaming. "Well . . . ," she said. "So?" She could barely get the words out. She slammed her notebooks pointlessly, burning with anger and shame. At the same moment, their teacher swung into the room.

"Good morning, everyone!" Ms Gettins said. "I hope you all enjoyed the homework! I certainly did. It's so lovely to rework those problems."

This was usually when Liv and Dallas rolled their eyes at each other. How could anyone like algebra that much? But there was no eye-rolling today. Liv stared down at her dirty, scratched-up worksheet. All her answers were probably wrong anyway.

Ms Gettins was floating up and down the aisles now, examining the homework. "Lovely, Jacob. Lovely, Margaret," she said. "Daniel, this one is not correct, my dear!"

Out of the corner of her eye, Liv could see Ms Gettins coming towards her. She shrank down in her seat. She didn't think she could stand anyone talking to her.

Ms Gettins stopped. Liv could hear the teacher's breathing. A woolly smell hung around her like a cloud. Liv thought she might choke.

Ms Gettins bent over. "Your homework is very messy, Liv." Her voice was quiet and patient.

She's treating me like a bomb that's about to go off, Liv thought. She raised her eyes to her teacher's face. She could see the foundation make-up patted over the wrinkles on Ms Gettins' cheeks.

The anger rose up in Liv like a demon she couldn't control. She stood suddenly, knocking her chair over. People looked over, startled.

"I don't care," Liv said loudly.

Ms Gettins straightened up and sighed. "I care, Liv. And I care that you are disrupting the lesson. Please go to the counsellor. Again."

The teacher turned away as Liv swept her books and papers into her bag. Her armpits were sweaty. She could make out the eyes of her classmates. They were all locked on her. Dallas, though, was looking firmly at the wall.

Stare! Stare at the freak! Liv wanted to shout at them all.

She tugged at the zip on her bag. It was stuck. *Forget it,* she thought. Liv swung the bag onto her back. Books and papers wobbled dangerously near the opening as she stepped out into the corridor.

She stood for a moment, letting the anger twist through her. It was fading away and leaving behind what it always did: a dull ache. Her legs didn't want to move, but she trudged towards the counsellor's office.

"Liv! What a surprise!" Mrs Kroger said as Liv walked into the office.

"Ha-ha," Liv muttered. She slumped into the familiar chair on the other side of the desk.

"Ms Gettins just buzzed down." Mrs Kroger put down her pen. "What happened this time? Did you throw anything?"

Liv shook her head.

"Well," Mrs Kroger said, "that's good."

"Look, I told Dallas I was sorry!" Liv burst out.

"I *accidentally* kicked the ball when Samin totally messed up in the game against Forest Park–"

"Let me guess," Mrs Kroger interrupted. "You hit Dallas with the ball and hurt her."

Liv nodded. "Yeah, but I *said*–"

"–you were sorry. I heard you." Mrs Kroger paused. "You know, Liv, most of the time, just saying you're sorry doesn't actually solve the problem." She held up a hand as Liv opened her mouth. "It does help. But people we hurt don't usually feel better until they can see we're taking responsibility for our actions *and* coming up with a solution."

Liv stared at her trainers. The counsellor's words floated by her ears. At least she wasn't in maths any more.

"In your case, it's gaining control over your temper," Mrs Kroger said.

Liv's head snapped up. Mrs Kroger was

leaning over her desk, her hands folded.

"There are some anger management classes that I can recommend," Mrs Kroger continued. "It would really be good for you, Liv."

Mrs Kroger slid a sheet of paper across the desk. Liv glanced at the list of classes and just shrugged. She didn't need some silly training on emotions.

Mrs Kroger sighed. "If you aren't willing to work on this, you will continue to have problems," she added. The counsellor slid her glasses down to the end of her nose and looked at Liv over the top.

Liv couldn't think what to say. Mrs Kroger tended to have this effect on her. She just stared you down with that over-the-glasses thing. It left Liv feeling like a worm squirming under a pin.

"Yeah," Liv muttered. "OK."

Mrs Kroger raised an eyebrow. "OK, what?"

"OK, I will work on my temper. But I can do it

on my own." Liv stood up. "Now can I go?"

Mrs Kroger nodded. "I'm serious, Liv. You're going to get into serious trouble eventually if you can't get a grip on your anger."

Liv fled from the room. Out in the corridor, she let out a big breath she didn't know she'd been holding. The last bell rang. Doors started banging open along the corridor. It was time for football practice.

Liv swung her rucksack onto her shoulder and walked towards the changing rooms. Kids were shouting and pushing all around her.

I will keep myself under control. I will, she thought. *I will do it.*

And this time, she meant to keep her promise.

CHAPTER 3

FOOTBALL FOCUS

Fifteen minutes later, Liv jogged out onto the pitch in her football kit. Just the feeling of the boots on her feet and the sun on her face made her feel better.

"Hey, Marie" she greeted the goalie.

"Hey," Marie said, smiling back.

Straight away, Liv looked around for Dallas, but then she remembered their fight. Her friend was standing a little way behind her. Liv waved nervously.

Dallas didn't do anything for a minute. Then she nodded. With relief, Liv jogged over to her. "Hey," she said.

"Hey," said Dallas.

Liv let out her breath. At least Dallas was speaking to her.

But before Liv could say anything else, Coach Davis clapped his hands. "Everybody, come over here for a minute," he shouted. "I've got a surprise for you all."

Excited whispers ran through the girls as they huddled around.

The coach looked at his clipboard and pushed his cap back on his balding head. "The League of Women in Athletics is sending you all on a trip to Lippert Stadium. You'll get to meet the Rangers, tour the changing rooms and fitness rooms and see the players on the pitch."

"The Rangers!" Chen shouted.

Liv and Dallas looked at each other with their eyes wide. Around them, their teammates started cheering and screaming. Ana was actually jumping up and down.

The Rangers were the new professional women's football team in their city. They had shot to fame with a perfect season with no defeats. The team was one of the best in the country – out of the women's *and* men's leagues.

Coach smiled. "All right, calm down. The LWA promotes young women's involvement in sport. This little field trip is a way to encourage you all to keep playing."

"When are we going?" Rose shouted.

"In two weeks. We'll take a bus and spend the afternoon there." Coach flipped the page on his clipboard and put it down on the bench. "But in the meantime, we have work to do. Let's start with some warm-up drills! Get going!"

Liv focused on the ball in front of her. She pushed all the drama from the school day out of her mind. She toed the ball up onto her laces and bounced it back and forth between her feet. The smack of the ball on her boots was almost calming.

"Lift those knees!" Coach shouted.

Engage your quads, Liv thought. Coach had taught her that last year. She concentrated on her thighs and brought her knees higher and higher. The muscles burned with effort, but she didn't let the rhythm of the bouncing ball falter.

Out of the corner of her eye, Liv could see Rose and Gabrielle slowing down. Their balls fell to the grass as their legs gave out, but Liv wasn't going to let that happen to her.

Sweat rolled down Liv's forehead. Her legs were starting to tire now. The burning feeling was spreading through her thighs. But she kept her eyes on the ball. She worked through the discomfort and pictured her muscles getting stronger.

Finally, Coach Davis blew his whistle.

Liv exhaled and let the ball drop to the ground.

"Nice, Liv!" Coach called. "You were the last one left."

Liv looked around at her teammates, who were all grinning at her. She hadn't even noticed that the other girls had stopped.

"OK, four-pass drills!" Coach yelled. "Move!"

They divided up quickly. Half the girls pulled bright yellow tops over their heads. The two teams would need to score in four passes or fewer. If they took more than that, they had to give the ball to the other side.

Liv ran into position. She felt good. The warm-up had left her mind focused and her muscles loose.

To start them off, Coach kicked the ball over to Jada on Liv's team. Rose ran over and was on her immediately. Jada tried to dribble around, but Rose nabbed the ball. She passed to Nevy.

27

Rija wasn't about to let the other team have possession so easily. Liv jogged down the pitch as her teammate wrestled it away from Nevy.

"Clear!" Liv shouted, and Rija booted the ball.

Liv grabbed it and started dribbling. Ana ran up beside her, ready to fight for the ball. Liv stopped and looked over towards Samin. But just as Ana moved to block the pass, Liv knocked it to Chen on the left instead.

Ana was caught off guard. She couldn't adjust fast enough to stop the ball.

Chen took it and made her way closer to the goal. Liv sprinted to the edge of the penalty box. Chen passed the ball back to her before Gabrielle could steal it away.

Spinning around Dallas, Liv eyed the goal. She could try to take the shot now. But she could see that Samin was open on the right. Their team only had one more pass. If she gave the ball to Samin, she would have to score.

Liv whacked the ball. Samin grabbed it and took the shot.

TUNK!

The ball hit the crossbar and flew off the pitch.

"Nice effort, Samin! Way to share the ball, Liv!" Coach shouted.

Liv huffed out a frustrated sigh and was going to say something to Samin. Then she remembered her promise to keep her temper under control. So Liv closed her mouth and pushed the anger away as the other team took the ball.

Just focus on football, she told herself.

But it wasn't easy.

CHAPTER 4

LOSING IT

"All right, let's move on to passing drills!"
Coach called. "Get a partner and line up."

Liv wiped the sweat from her forehead as
the girls started pairing off. She had managed to
score in the last minute of the four-pass drill, but
it wasn't enough for her team to win. The score
ended 6–4. Without thinking, she clenched her jaw.

Stay calm, Liv reminded herself. She tried to
relax as she walked up to Dallas. "Partners?"
she asked.

Dallas gave a nod.

They backed apart and joined the double line of partners facing each other. Coach walked down the line, dropping a ball in front of each pair. Dallas kicked the ball to Liv, who tapped it back with a *thwack*.

After a few silent passes, Liv asked, "Did you make it through the rest of maths?"

"Yeah. How was Mrs Kroger?" Dallas' voice was distant but friendly.

"Same," Liv replied. "You know, intense."

"Oh yeah." Dallas tilted her head down and pretended to be looking over the top of a pair of glasses.

Liv laughed as she hit the ball back to her friend. She knew things would work out fine, just like they always did. She never wanted to be anywhere but here in the bright sun, with her team.

Then a voice floated over the general chatter. "That girl is like a pit bull."

Someone else said, "Totally. I honestly can't believe she hasn't bitten anyone yet."

The first girl laughed.

Liv's hands went sweaty. Those girls were talking about her. She just knew it. She leaned forward and looked down the line.

Rija and Rose were laughing. They saw Liv looking and stopped. Rija flicked her long hair and smiled.

A mixture of shame and fury rose up in Liv's throat. In the back of her mind, she heard Mrs Kroger's voice. *You're going to get into serious trouble eventually . . .*

But the sight of Rija's smirk made Liv stop caring what Mrs Kroger thought.

She started towards Rija.

"Liv!" Dallas shouted. "She didn't mean it!"

Liv felt Dallas grab the back of her top,
but she pulled away. She kept stomping forward.

"I heard what you said!" Liv shouted into Rija's
face. Then she shoved her hard with both hands.

The minute her hands touched the other girl,
Liv knew she'd gone too far. Rija fell backwards
onto the ground. Everyone around them gasped.

Liv sucked in her breath. "Oh, I'm sorry! I'm so
sorry!" She tried to reach down to pull Rija up. But
the other girl, still on the ground, turned away.

"You'd better come with me, Liv," Coach Davis
said. He had come up behind them.

Just looking at his face told Liv two things.
One, he'd seen what had happened. And two,
she was in bigger trouble than she'd ever been in
before.

Liv couldn't look at anyone – not Rija on the
ground, not Dallas, not her teammates. She just
followed the coach off the pitch and tried to ignore

the other girls' silent stares.

Coach didn't speak until they had reached the changing room doors. Then he sank down on one of the old black folding chairs that always sat in the corridor. He motioned for Liv to take the other one. Liv carefully sat, as if the chair might explode. Like her life seemed to have.

But unlike all the other adults she had faced in the past two days, Coach didn't fix her with a hard stare. Instead, he sank his head into his hands and looked down at his trainers. He sat that way for a long time.

Finally, Liv asked, "Um, Coach? Are you OK?"

Coach didn't answer for a moment, and then he lifted his head. His usually cheerful face was sad. He took off his glasses and rubbed his nose. Without them, his face looked strange. Liv felt so ashamed.

"Coach, I'm really sorry," she began.

He held up his hand.

"I've heard it before, Liv," he said. "I've heard 'Coach, I'm sorry,' and 'It was her fault.' I have to say, I'm sick of it." His voice rose sharply on the last sentence. He stood. "Today was the last straw. Today you deliberately hurt another player."

Coach stared at the opposite wall. When he spoke again, his voice was low. "Liv, today is going to have consequences."

Then he walked off down the corridor, leaving her alone.

* * *

That night, Liv sat in her room. She tried to focus on maths, but she couldn't stop thinking about what had happened. Rija's face, her mouth open in surprise as she fell to the ground. Dallas looking away. Coach's tired eyes.

An email dinged on her phone. The subject line read, "Meeting requested 3 October: Liv Sutcliffe."

Liv didn't have to be a genius to see this coming.

To: Liv Sutcliffe, Michael Sutcliffe and Coach
Andrew Davis

The administration department at Campbell Middle
School kindly requests a meeting with the above pupil,
parent or guardian, and involved teacher or coach.
Mrs Kroger, guidance counsellor, and Mrs Bishop, head
teacher, will attend. Consequences of recent behaviour
during school activities will be discussed.
The meeting will take place in Mrs Kroger's office
on 3 October at 3.45 p.m.

That was tomorrow.

Liv put down her phone and stared at the
wall. She could feel heavy sadness tugging at
the corners of her mouth. She wished for a time
machine. She wished she could travel back to
the moment when she shoved Rija and erase it all.
She wished it so badly.

But no time machine appeared, and tomorrow
Liv would have to face the consequences.

CHAPTER 5

THE MEETING

Liv and her dad knocked on Mrs Kroger's door on Wednesday after school.

"Come in," Mrs Kroger called.

As soon as she opened the door, Liv knew that Mrs Kroger, Coach Davis and Mrs Bishop had been talking about her. She could see her file open on Mrs Kroger's desk. Coach was sitting next to Mrs Bishop, the headmistress. She gave Liv a friendly smile.

Dad nudged her forward, and Liv sat down on the very edge of the extra chair they'd squeezed into the room. Dad sat beside her and folded his hands tightly in his lap. She stole a quick glance at his face. He looked as nervous as she was.

"Liv, please remember that we are here to help you, not punish you," Mrs Kroger began. "We are very concerned. You have such difficulty controlling your temper, both on and off the football pitch. And yesterday, you hurt another pupil."

Liv nodded, but she felt as if she could hardly breathe. She kept taking in air in little gulps.

Mrs Bishop leaned forward. "Liv, violence is unacceptable. Really, you should be suspended from school. However–" She nodded at Coach.

"You're suspended from the team," Coach said. "I hate to do it, Liv."

The room was so hot. Sweat trickled down the sides of Liv's face. She wanted to wipe it away, but her arms felt heavy. "How long?" she whispered.

"The rest of the year," Mrs Bishop said.

Liv's chest grew tighter. On her other side, she saw Dad's back slump as if the wind had been knocked out of him.

She heard Coach reading out a list of rules, but it sounded far away. They were rules to keep her from her team, girls who were like her sisters.

"You are not to take to the pitch for any practice or matches, although you are permitted to watch them," Coach said. "You are not to receive any coaching. You must hand in your team kit and any other team equipment that you have. You are not to participate in any team outings–"

Liv's head shot up. Team outings! The Lippert Stadium trip!

"Wait!" she cried.

Coach stopped.

"You mean I can't go to Lippert? I can't meet the Rangers?" Liv asked. Her voice was small and shaky in the quiet room.

Coach glanced at Mrs Bishop, who shook her head. "I'm afraid not, Liv," Mrs Bishop said gently. "That's what *suspended* means."

"Oh. Got it, got it." Liv nodded rapidly as if she understood, as if she were a puppet. She needed to get out of there. "OK, thank you." She stood up so fast she stumbled backwards. Dad caught her arm.

"Thank you," he said, nodding awkwardly at the school staff.

Liv left the room, trying not to cry. She walked quickly through the empty corridors and burst out through the front doors. She let out her breath and sucked in a lungful of the crisp fall air.

"I'm off the team!" Liv said. The words sounded unbelievable to her. "I'm off the team!"

"I know," her dad said. "I heard."

Liv glanced back at Dad. He was staring at the ground, rubbing his chin.

"Dad–" Liv started.

"I've gotta get back to the shop, Livvy," he interrupted. "You go on home. I'll try to be there in time for dinner." He paused. "I'm really sorry about all this. I wish I could help, but I . . . I just don't know how."

She watched Dad start the pick-up truck and drive away. The anger swept over her again. She balled up her fists and shrieked into the air. She punched the metal post next to her.

It hurt – really badly. She gasped and doubled over, cradling her fist against her stomach. Slowly, she sank down onto the pavement.

Liv deserved the suspension. She knew that. But the question was: what was she going to do now?

CHAPTER 6

GETTING HELP

Liv shivered in her jacket as she trudged along the pavement towards home. Everything had gone wrong after she pushed Rija.

Almost as bad as getting suspended from the team was Dallas. Liv's best friend had completely avoided her at school. And she wasn't responding to any texts. Liv thought she could almost handle not being on the team if she still had Dallas as her friend.

Except her temper had even ruined that.

Liv walked past the bakery and the architect's offices. Then the corner with the church. Normally Liv would try to think about what she wanted to eat when she got home after these long, cold walks. But tonight she didn't have the heart. She didn't have any heart left at all.

The Healing Space was next. It was an old, cream-coloured house next to the church. Dad said it had been the vicar's house once. Now it was a yoga studio and therapist's treatment rooms run by a lady who did essential oils. Weird, hippie stuff like that.

Suddenly Liv stopped. A sign board stood on the pavement. She'd probably walked past it a thousand times. The Healing Space put posters on it to advertise their different activities. She had never looked at it. Tonight, though, two words caught her eye.

Anger Problems?

She certainly had anger problems. Liv moved

closer to the poster.

Anger Problems? Worried? Depressed? Come to our Mindfulness Workshop on Saturday, 9.00–10.00 a.m. to learn to control your emotions through mindfulness. Certified mindfulness coach Julie Cleveland will lead you through a series of exercises. No experience necessary. $15, pay at the door.

Liv had no idea what the poster was talking about. What was mindfulness? It sounded like more hippie stuff. Still, the poster said "control your emotions". She wanted to control her anger.

Liv dug a pen out of her rucksack and wrote *Saturday, 9.00* on her arm. It wasn't like she had a lot of better solutions.

* * *

Liv hung back in the doorway of a large octagon-shaped room. Several people were already sitting on the floor in the middle of a shabby orange rug. They were all adults.

"Hello!" a big, tall woman greeted her. "Are you here for the mindfulness workshop?"

The woman wore glasses that made her eyes look huge. The place smelled like spicy oil.

Liv stepped back. "Um, I – I," she stammered, trying to think of an excuse to leave.

"Welcome!" the woman said. Liv had the strange feeling that the woman knew she wanted to go. "I'm Julie."

"I'm Liv," Liv said nervously.

"Find a seat, Liv," Julie told her. "We'll get started soon."

Liv crept into the room and chose a spot on the rug by the wall. She looked around. The place had old wooden floors and sunlight streaming through dusty windows. Plants sat everywhere. Liv shifted uneasily on her bit of rug.

Julie beamed at the room. "Thank you all for coming to our mindfulness workshop. I hope you find the exercises helpful."

She switched on a stereo near her and the sound of rushing wind filled the room. Liv sneaked a quick glance around her. Everyone else was sitting cross-legged, with their eyes closed. Liv arranged herself the same way and squeezed her eyes shut.

"Our emotions are a part of us," Julie said softly. "They make us human. But sometimes, it feels as if our emotions are controlling us. We don't want to be a victim of our emotions."

Liv tried to focus on Julie's words. She could hear the woman next to her breathing. She tried not to shift around on the rug.

"Mindfulness helps us to be aware of our emotions and, eventually, to control them," Julie said. "Let's start with a simple breathing exercise. I call it square breathing. Breathe in for the count of five, then hold for five, then out for five. Then in for five. I'll talk you through it."

Breathing? Just breathing is the magic cure? Liv

thought. But she breathed all the time!

Liv peeked through one eye at Julie, who happened to be looking at her. Julie smiled and winked. Liv quickly shut her eyes again. She'd never felt so awkward.

"Let's all try it together," Julie said gently. She started counting. "One, two, three, four, five."

Liv let out a sigh, but she tried to match her inhaling with Julie's counting. "And hold two, three, four, five. Now out two, three, four, five. And hold two, three, four, five."

Liv listened to the rush of her own breath in her ears. Julie's voice was strangely calming. Slowly, the darkness behind her eyelids started to seem less weird and more comfortable. It was almost as if there was only Julie's voice and her own breathing. . . .

At the end of the hour, Liv made her way towards Julie. "Well, hello," Julie greeted her as she unplugged the stereo and wound up its cord.

"What did you think of the class?"

"I liked it," Liv said. Yes, it had been strange, but she did feel a little better. "But . . ."

Julie looked up from her cord-wrapping. "Yes?" she asked.

"The poster for this class said you could help with, um, anger problems?" Liv's face was burning.

"That's right," Julie replied.

"I don't understand what the breathing has to do with it," Liv blurted out.

"Ah." Julie studied Liv for a moment. "I'm guessing you're a girl who might be in need of a little help. Do you want to tell me your story, and I'll see if I can do anything?"

Liv stayed quiet. *No one else has been able to help, so why would this stranger be able to?* she asked herself.

But then the thought of not playing football this season flashed through Liv's mind. Maybe, *maybe,* if she could show Coach she really was working on her anger, he might lift the suspension.

She took a deep breath. Standing there in front of the windows, she poured out the whole awful story.

Julie nodded when Liv had finally finished. "Liv, I hear you," she said. "I hear that you've struggled with controlling your temper. The good news is that these mindfulness exercises can help with anger. But you will have to learn them and practise."

"OK," Liv said. "OK, I will." She felt as if she'd do anything if someone could help her.

"So, I have an idea," Julie said. "You seem like a pretty talented footballer. My son, Damien, wants to get on the football team this autumn. He's eight. How about we do a trade? I'll come to your house and give you a private anger management coaching session. And you can give Damien some football training."

Liv felt a smile crack her face for what seemed like the first time in a year. "Yeah," she said. "I can do that."

"It's a date, then," Julie said. "How about next Saturday, your house, two o'clock?"

Liv nodded. "I'll be ready."

CHAPTER 7

NEW SKILLS

"OK, Damien! For trials, they're going to want you to take a couple of shots on goal, so let's practise," Liv said.

It was Saturday afternoon, and Damien had been running drills with Liv in the back garden for half an hour. Julie said they'd play first, and then she and Liv would work together.

Julie sat next to the patio table. Her face was shaded by the green umbrella as she drank a glass of iced tea and talked to Dad.

Liv stood in front of the little goal. Damien dribbled through a line of cones she had set up. When he turned around the last one, he kicked the ball.

It rolled slowly past the corner of the goal. Liv tapped it back.

"Shoot hard and straight. That's what the coaches will want to see," she called to him. "Try kicking it on your laces."

Damien nodded and ran forward. He shot the ball straight past her as she dived for it.

"Nice!" Liv shouted, getting back to her feet. "Really nice! I didn't have a chance of stopping that one."

Damien grinned. "Wow! I've never kicked it that hard before."

"Well, when you get on the team, you're going to be doing a lot more of that hard kicking," Liv replied, slapping him a high five.

Damien set up for another try. Liv smiled. It felt good to be kicking around a football again. And it felt good to be coaching Damien. It was pretty cool that she knew enough to teach a younger player.

"OK, come here," Liv said after Damien had scored a few more goals. "I'm going to show you something that the coaches will love. It's a freestyle move."

"What's freestyle?" Damien asked.

"They're like little tricks," Liv explained. "They're not much good on the pitch when you're playing, but they're great for ball-handling skills. It shows you know how to use your feet."

Liv dropped the ball on the grass. Damien's big eyes were locked on her.

"OK, this is called the footstall. It's one of the first tricks I learned," Liv said. "It's where you keep the ball balanced on your foot."

She nudged her toe under the ball. It popped up onto her laces. She lifted her leg and balanced the ball between her shoe and her shin.

"You want to keep the ball here. Lift your toes up to help trap it. Then try moving your leg." She slowly moved her leg back and forth. The ball stayed put. She dropped it off her shoe. "OK, your turn."

Damien tried to pop the ball up from the ground like Liv had, but it rolled off his foot. He tried again. "You make it look so easy," he said.

Liv nodded. "Maybe it looks easy now, but this trick took me forever to learn. I kept dropping it, just like you."

Damien looked up. "Really?"

"Yeah, really," Liv replied. "And you'll make it look easy too eventually. You just can't give up. That's the only way to master football. One of my first coaches told me that. Here, try this."

She put the ball right on Damien's laces. He lifted his toes and balanced the ball for a full two seconds.

"When you get the hang of that, you can move on to something more advanced," Liv told him.

She scooped the ball up with her shoe, balanced it, and kicked it up. She bounced the ball between her feet. Then she caught it on her foot again.

"The key is to not kick it up too high or hit it too hard," Liv explained. "That'll make it harder to catch it when you want."

"Yeah." Damien nodded his head up and down. "You're a good teacher, Liv."

"Oh, um . . . thanks," Liv said. She patted Damien on the shoulder.

They went back to practising. Damien's forehead wrinkled as he focused. He was balancing the ball for four seconds now. He even managed to tap it up once.

"See? You're getting it," Liv said. "You just have to keep practising."

Damien nodded again. He was already putting the ball back on his shoe.

From the patio, Julie clapped. "Way to go, champ. You're looking like a football pro. But it's my turn to do the coaching now," Julie said. "OK, Liv, come on over here."

Liv let out a sigh as she walked to the patio. She wished she could spend the whole day working on football skills with Damien.

Julie pulled out a chair for Liv. They both sat down, facing each other.

"All right," Julie said. "I want you to start by closing your eyes."

Liv glanced over at Dad, and he gave her an encouraging smile. She closed her eyes, still feeling silly. But she was going to try. She'd never given up on the pitch, and she wasn't going to give up now.

"To control anger, we have to accept anger," Julie said. "I want you to think of the last time you were really angry."

That was easy enough. Liv pictured herself pushing Rija.

"Let yourself feel the anger again," Julie continued. "It's OK. You're safe here. Now I want you to think about how the anger feels. Does it feel hot? Or cold?"

Liv felt a burning knot in her chest. Her hands itched. "It feels hot. And tight."

"Right, good. Where in your body do you feel the anger?" Julie asked.

"In my chest. My hands. My face." It was like angry little prickles underneath Liv's skin that were trying to get out.

"Very good," Julie said. "Now, I want you to tell the anger that it's OK."

"What?" Liv said, opening her eyes. To her surprise, Dad had his eyes closed too.

Julie smiled. "It's OK to feel angry," she said. "It's normal. Humans get angry sometimes. So tell your anger, 'It's OK. You're normal.'"

Liv closed her eyes again. Even though it felt weird, she focused on her anger. *It's OK,* she told it. *You're normal.*

"Now, it's time to say goodbye to the anger," Julie continued. "Let the anger go and watch it move away."

Liv breathed out. She imagined a red ball drifting away from her, bouncing into the air. It grew smaller until she couldn't see it any more.

Liv opened her eyes. She felt peaceful and calm. Julie was smiling at her. So was Dad.

"So, Liv, this is an exercise you can do anywhere, anytime," Julie said. "I've helped you through it, but you can do it by yourself. When you feel the anger coming up, find it in your body. Tell it that it's there, and that it's OK. Then let it go. And do your breathing."

"It'll work, Liv," Damien piped up. Liv twisted around in surprise. He was standing behind her chair, bouncing the ball. She'd almost forgotten he was there. "Mum's exercises always work. You just have to keep practising."

Liv smiled. *Keep practising!* Just what she'd said to him. Liv thought back to her last football practice, when she'd kept up the ball longer than anyone. She'd never had trouble putting in the hard work to be a better player. If she thought of the mindfulness exercises as just another skill to master . . . maybe they wouldn't seem so strange.

"Thanks, Julie. This was good stuff," Dad said, standing up as Julie gathered her things.

"My pleasure. And, Liv, let me know how it all goes, OK?" Julie said. She started to leave, but Damien held back.

"I'm still nervous about trials," Damien said in a small voice.

Liv looked at him. "You're going to be fine! Just

remember what we worked on today." She paused. "Do you . . . want me to come with you? I could help you warm up before you start."

Damien's face lit up. "Yeah! Can you? Can she, Mum?"

"Of course," Julie said. "That's so kind of you, Liv. Thank you."

Liv gave Damien one final high five before they left. Then she headed inside. She wanted to start practising her mindfulness exercise straight away.

She wasn't sure if it'd work when she actually got angry. But she was going to give it her best shot.

CHAPTER 8

PRACTICE MAKES PERFECT

Damien crowded close to Liv's side when they walked onto the football pitch for trials the next afternoon. Julie had dropped them off while she went to park. Boys were standing around and stretching. The coaches stood in a clump to one side, flicking through piles of papers.

"These kids look big," Damien whispered.

"They're the same size as you," Liv told him. "Come on! Let's warm up. You'll feel better when you start moving."

Suddenly, Liv spotted Rija on the other side of the pitch. She was with a little boy who had the same dark hair and eyes. Liv thought he must be her younger brother.

Liv's stomach flipped at the sight of Rija. But she turned her back, snagged a nearby ball and started passing back and forth with Damien.

"Remember to get your laces under it," she called to him. "Be confident. Attack the ball and follow through."

Damien nodded and knocked the ball over. It hit her shoe with a hard *thwack*.

"Good!" Liv said.

"And that's good advice," someone said from behind her.

Liv turned around. "Coach!"

Coach Davis smiled. "Pete is trying out today," he said, motioning to the boy by his side. "He's my middle son."

"Oh! Hi," Liv said to Pete. She wondered if Coach was still angry with her. "I'm here with Damien. He's the son of my . . . friend."

Damien waved. "Liv's been coaching me," he said. "She's awesome."

Liv felt her cheeks get warm. Coach raised his eyebrows. "Well, that's a nice vote of confidence." He gave them a little nod as he and Pete walked away. "See you around."

"All right, let's get into a line, please!" one of the coaches shouted.

Liv gave Damien a pat on the back. "Go get 'em," she said. "You're going to be great." They high-fived, and he jogged over to the line.

As the kids started trials, everyone else walked off the pitch. Rija noticed Liv as she came over to the touchline. She crossed her arms.

"I didn't know you were even allowed to be on football pitches any more," Rija said.

Liv didn't say anything. She focused on breathing in and out, just like she had practised last night.

"Who's that little boy?" Rija asked.

Liv watched as Damien ran up to the ball and booted it straight into the goal. She smiled. "He's my teacher's kid. I've been coaching him."

"Oh, wow. Really?" Rija threw her long black hair over her shoulder. "She actually trusts you with him? Like, isn't she worried you're going to flip out and beat him up?"

The anger rose up strong in Liv, coloured bright red. It came so fast and strong she almost staggered back with the force of it. She turned towards Rija. She wanted to yell, to tell her how wrong she was.

But a voice inside her spoke up.

Breathe! it said. It was Julie's voice. *Do your breathing. When you feel the anger coming up, find it in your body. Tell it that it's there, and that it's OK.*

Liv took a step back. She closed her eyes. She didn't care how silly she looked.

She could feel the anger inside, fighting like a wild horse on the end of a rope. It was hard to hold back.

Liv breathed. In five. Hold five. Out five. Hold five. Where was the anger? In her chest, definitely. And her hands.

Anger, you're OK, Liv thought. She felt the wild horse relax a little. *Anger is normal to feel.*

She kept breathing. She imagined carefully letting go of the rope. The horse looked back at her.

Then, it galloped away. She watched it go over the horizon. She opened her eyes.

The anger was gone.

"It worked!" Liv burst out.

Rija glared at her. "What are you talking about? What worked? You are seriously weird." Rija shook her head and stomped away.

"Actually, I could ask the same question, Liv."
Coach got up from a nearby bench. She hadn't
even noticed him sitting there.

"Oh, I've been taking some lessons in . . .
um . . . anger management, with this coach,
Julie. She's Damien's mum," Liv said. She felt a
bit awkward talking about this to Coach, but she
plunged ahead anyway. She explained Julie's
techniques. "So when I felt really mad at Rija,
I did my exercises and it worked."

Coach nodded slowly. "I heard what Rija said.
I can understand why you felt angry. But I can't
tell you how glad I am that you didn't act on it."
He looked at Liv. "Nice work."

Liv smiled. Coach had said it in just the same
way he used to when she'd made a good move
during practice.

* * *

"How'd the trials go?" Dad asked later.

He stood at the cooker, mixing cocoa powder into milk in a saucepan. Liv sat at the table. She cradled her chin in her hands as she watched him.

"Good! Damien made the team!" Liv replied. And he'd given her a huge hug afterwards, which felt like all the thanks she'd ever need. Liv took a deep breath. "And something else happened too."

She told the story of what Rija had said, how she'd controlled herself, and what Coach had said.

Dad listened silently. When Liv finished, he put a mug of cocoa down in front of her and sank into a chair with his own cup. He took a long sip.

"You did good, Livvy," he said finally. "Coach thinks so too. He told you that." Dad stared down into his cocoa. "You know, you might consider asking Coach for another chance. Now that he's seen that you're seriously working on your temper this time."

"Really?" Liv said. "Do you really think he'd give me another try?"

Dad held up his hand. "Don't get me wrong, you still have a lot of work to do," he said. "Your anger issues aren't going to be solved in one day. You have to keep at it. No more trips to the counsellor for misbehaving in lessons. Keep going to your sessions with Julie. But if you tell Coach that's what you're willing to do, he might see how serious you are."

"Oh, I am! I mean, I will!" Liv gulped down her cocoa. Maybe Dad was right. She could ask, at least. She could try.

CHAPTER 9

ON THE BENCH

Liv thought she had never done anything harder than walking up to the team bench at the start of the home match against Mason. She stared straight ahead as the whispers spread around her. Everyone knew about the suspension of course.

Let them whisper, Liv thought. *I'm making changes. And I'm going to prove it.*

Liv planted herself at one end of the bench. Dallas and Chen were at the other end – with Rija.

The starting lineup were gathered around Coach near the centre circle. Gabrielle looked over at Liv, then said something to Coach. He looked over too.

Liv tried a small wave. Coach waved back, and Liv exhaled. She could stay. She'd crossed the first hurdle.

"Hey," Chen called softly down the bench.

"Hey!" Liv called back. She tried to make eye contact with Dallas. Her friend gave a tight-lipped smile. That was something.

The Mason players jogged onto the pitch. Their bright red uniforms popped against the green turf. Samin was taking the kick-off. Liv's feet itched to be out there as the ref blew his whistle.

Samin tapped the ball over to Nevy on the wing. She took the ball and made a quick move down the left side of the pitch.

The Mason midfielder was on her. The other girl shoved her foot forward for the tackle, but she kicked it out instead.

The assistant ref raised her flag. It was the Falcons' throw-in.

Samin ran to the touchline and flicked the ball back into play. Jada took it and started to dribble.

But a Mason player sprinted up. She bumped her shoulder into Jada and got her foot around the ball. She booted it down the pitch.

Mason players passed the ball smoothly across the grass. They were rushing towards the goal now.

Liv's legs bounced nervously as she watched. She wanted to help her team, but all she could do was cheer them on. "Fight them off, Falcons!" she shouted.

Ana looked towards the bench, surprised by Liv's voice. The charging Mason striker took advantage of Ana's pause and darted past her. The striker smacked the ball at the goal.

But Marie jumped forward. The Falcons

goalkeeper wrapped her arms around the ball and then threw it to Jada.

Ana glanced over at Liv again. She whispered something to Rose as they jogged down the pitch. Liv felt her face grow warm. She tried not to care what they were saying.

Instead Liv glanced down the bench at the others. Rija was staring right at her. She was mouthing something. *Psycho.*

Liv felt the red anger swoop through her. She inhaled sharply.

Liv squeezed her eyes shut. *You've done this once before. You can do it again,* she told herself.

But it wasn't any easier. The burning, prickly anger rushed through her and made it hard to focus. She kept thinking about all her teammates' whispering. They were all staring at her, she was sure of it.

Liv forced herself to breathe in for five. Hold

for five. Then out for five. She found the anger inside her.

It's OK, anger, she thought. *You're there. But now it's time to say goodbye.* She imagined the ball of anger bouncing out of her chest. She immediately felt lighter.

Liv blinked her eyes open. She'd done it. She had controlled her anger – for the second time in just a few days.

She looked over at Rija. The other girl was talking to Chen now. Liv took a careful breath. The anger really was gone.

She sat up straighter. Dallas noticed and gave her a questioning look. Liv just smiled.

Out on the pitch, Gabrielle made a powerful kick. The ball soared over the players' heads.

Samin ran forward to take it and made a one-touch pass to Nevy on the left. Nevy twisted past two defenders and dribbled closer to Mason's goal. She snapped it back to Samin.

Samin was ready. She charged towards the goal.

With a flick of her foot, Samin sneaked the ball under the goalkeeper's outstretched arms. Goal!

Liv jumped and cheered along with the Falcons players and fans. As she clapped, Dallas walked over and sat on Liv's end of the bench.

"Hey, Liv," Dallas said slowly. "I don't know what you were doing earlier, but . . . it seems like something is different with you."

Liv felt a wave of relief wash over her. Dallas was speaking to her. She hadn't got angry at Rija.

"Yeah, something is different," Liv said.

Dallas smiled, a real smile, and put an arm around her. "I'm glad," she said.

* * *

The half-time whistle blew, and the team jogged over to the touchline. It had been tough, but the Falcons managed to keep their 1–0 lead.

As the girls grabbed their water bottles, Coach Davis came to the bench. Liv sat up extra tall.

"Glad you turned up, Liv," Coach said.

"I wanted to support the team, even though I can't play," Liv said. "And Coach, I know you saw that I'm working on my temper problem. I've kept on with my lessons with my mindfulness coach."

"A mindfulness coach?" Dallas said next to her. "Whoa, that sounds fancy."

Liv gave her friend a nudge. "But it is helping," she said.

"That's good, Liv. Very good," Coach replied. "I'm glad to hear you're sticking with it."

Now was the time. Liv asked, "Do you . . . think I could come back?" Before Coach could say anything, she went on in a rush. She listed all the other things she was going to do.

Coach frowned thoughtfully. "I don't know if you can rejoin the team yet, Liv. It's not just my decision to make. But I am impressed by the work you're doing." He paused and smiled. "I'll talk to Mrs Bishop. How does that sound?"

"Yes! Thank you!" Liv said, almost shouting the words.

"Oh! What about the Lippert trip next Tuesday?" Dallas added, getting excited. "Maybe you can go!"

Coach held up a hand. "Hang on," he said. "I said I'll talk to Mrs Bishop. That's all."

Liv nodded. "Of course, I understand. Thank you, Coach." She looked over at the rest of the Falcons. The girls were huddled together, doing stretches.

Liv knew that, no matter what the headmistress and Coach decided, she was committed to making a change. For her team, and for herself.

CHAPTER 10

GOALS

It was like being in a dream. Two weeks ago, Liv had been miserable and suspended from the team.

Now, she was wearing her blue Falcons uniform. And she was standing on the pitch at Lippert Stadium.

The pitch was huge. The gleaming white stands seemed to rise up around them like walls. The turf was thick and emerald-green. Liv could almost hear the shouts of the fans in the empty stands.

"Let's warm up, everyone!" Coach called as he threw a few balls onto the pitch. "Passing!"

The team spread out across the pitch. Dallas started off with a quick pass to Ana, who shot it to Marie, who kicked it to Chen. Then Chen sent the ball spinning towards Liv. She quickly stopped it and whacked it to Nevy.

Liv smiled. The passing felt good and rhythmic. It was like an old melody she'd just remembered.

The ball soared back towards Liv. This time it was in the air. She ran forward and stopped it with a chest bump.

The ball fell to the grass in front of her. She shot it straight to Rose. It made a satisfying *thwack* against her boot.

The ball passed smoothly between the players, rolling across the perfect pitch. Soon Coach called for them to move on to a dribbling warm-up.

As the girls arranged themselves, Liv searched for Rija. There was something she had been meaning to do. She jogged over to her teammate.

"Hey," Liv said quietly.

Rija glanced at Liv and looked away.

Liv swallowed hard. For a minute, it felt as if she couldn't make the words come out. "Listen. I'm really sorry I pushed you. That was wrong."

Rija kept staring at the stands. Then she nodded and dribbled down the pitch. That was all.

Well, Liv thought as she ran to grab her own ball. *I don't think we're going to be best friends.* But she had apologized – and she'd meant it, and she was making changes. That was the important thing.

After four laps of dribbling around the pitch, the Rangers appeared. They jogged out from the changing rooms in their practice kit.

The Falcons stopped and stared. Then Liv started clapping. Soon everyone was cheering too.

The Rangers grinned and waved as they spread out in front of them. The professional players were tall and strong. Their hair was pulled back in ponytails just like the younger players.

The Falcons quickly kicked their balls to the touchline. Liv and Dallas shared a smile as they got into their positions. Liv could hardly believe it. They were about to practice with the Rangers!

The older players grinned at the younger ones. "You girls ready to lose?" the midfielder, Jackie Wallace, called out.

"Sorry, did you mean *you're* ready to lose?" Rose called back, which Liv thought was pretty brave.

"Let's go!" one of the Rangers shouted.

Before Liv could react, a midfielder had shot the ball past her. Nevy tried to block it, but all of a sudden the ball was across the pitch.

Nevy laughed. "I can't even see the ball go!" she called to Liv.

The Rangers striker slowed way down and gently tapped the ball along. Liv knew that she was giving Jada a chance to tackle.

Normally, Liv would be annoyed if someone went easy on them. But she felt OK when the Rangers did it. They *were* a lot better than the Falcons, after all!

Jada took the opportunity and grabbed the ball. She shot to Samin, who gained control with a Rangers defender only half-trying to wrestle it away.

Liv looked around and realized she was clear. "Samin!" she shouted, running down the pitch.

A Rangers player was on Liv in a second, but the woman gave her a grin and stepped back a bit.

Samin booted the ball, and Liv swooped on it. She tapped it forward.

This was it. This was her chance to score in front of professional players – and in Lippert

Stadium! Liv felt her excitement build. She dribbled closer.

A Rangers defender darted forward. Liv used one foot to quickly push the ball against her other leg and then flicked it up. The ball flew over the other player in an arc. It was a risky, showy freestyle move. But Liv ran around her opponent, got control of the ball, and kept dribbling forward.

"Nice!" someone called.

The goal was in reach now. Liv could see the white net fluttering, just waiting for the ball. Her vision narrowed. Her heartbeat pounded in her ears. She got into position.

Now. Do it now! she told herself.

The Rangers goalie spread her hands wide and bounced on her feet. Liv drew back to take the shot.

Then she kicked – and missed the ball entirely.

Liv stumbled backwards with the force of the kick as her leg swept through the air, leaving the ball sitting on the grass. She fell to the ground.

Both teams laughed as a Rangers player ran in and booted the ball to the other side of the pitch. Liv stood up. The familiar tightness was blooming in her chest. She clenched her fists, then stopped.

It's OK, anger. She closed her eyes and took two deep breaths.

The tightness in her chest went away.

Liv opened her eyes and looked around the pitch. Dallas held her hand up in a high five. Liv held her hand up too.

"Liv! Are you asleep?" Nevy yelled.

Liv snapped out of her thoughts in time to see the ball shooting towards her. She ran alongside it and quickly stopped the ball with a tap. Then she lost it just as quickly as another Rangers defender sprinted in and nabbed it away.

Liv laughed and threw her arms up in the air in a "what can I do?" gesture. The ball disappeared down the pitch. The Rangers players passed it along with a speed Liv could only hope to have one day.

But for now she'd started working on herself. She was back on the team. It was a beautiful day, and she was playing with professional footballers.

I'll take it, Liv thought. *I'll take today. And we'll see what happens tomorrow.*

ABOUT the AUTHOR

Emma Carlson Berne has written more than eighty books for children and young adults, including novels, histories, biographies and several Sport Stories. She lives in Ohio, USA, with her husband and three little boys. When she isn't writing, Emma loves horse riding and walking in the woods.

GLOSSARY

consequence something that happens as a result of a person's actions

drill repetitive exercise that helps you learn a specific skill

footstall balance a football on the top of your foot while your leg is in the air

mindfulness practice of being aware of your feelings without judging them

striker player whose main responsibility is to score; also called a forward

suspend stop someone from taking part in an activity for a period of time

unsporting behaviour that isn't fair and respectful

winger player who plays on the left or right side of the pitch and creates scoring opportunities

DISCUSSION QUESTIONS

1. In your own words, summarize how Liv felt when she went to the mindfulness class. Talk about why you think she decided to stay for the whole session.

2. Compare Liv at the beginning of the story to at the end. How is her behaviour the same? How is it different? What caused the changes? Make sure you use evidence from the text to support your answer.

3. Imagine the Falcons' next game. Do you think Liv will be able to control her temper? Discuss why or why not.

WRITING PROMPTS

1. Players on a team depend on each other. List five qualities of a good teammate. Then write a paragraph arguing whether or not Liv fits that description at the beginning of the story.

2. This story is told from Liv's perspective, but how do the other girls feel about Liv's behaviour? Rewrite Chapter 4 from either Dallas' or Rija's point of view.

3. Whether it's controlling your temper or dribbling a football, learning a new skill takes practice. Write three paragraphs about a time you learned something new. Describe the process. Was it easy or hard? How did you overcome challenges?

UNUSUAL & UNIQUE
FOOTBALL PITCHES

Travel around the world to discover one-of-a-kind football stadiums and fascinating facts!

HNK Trogir's pitch in Croatia is between two 15th century fortresses! The tower of St Marco is behind one goal and Kamerlengo Castle is behind the other.

Kick the ball around in the mountains at Ottmar Hitzfeld Stadium in the Swiss village of Gspon. This pitch sits in the middle of the Alps and can only be reached by cable car. Players say that anywhere between five to ten balls are lost over the cliffside during each match.

Do some shopping before the game at Adidas Futsal Park. The pitch is located on the roof of a tall department store building in Tokyo, Japan.

In Marina Bay, Singapore, you can play football on the water! A steel platform called The Float holds an entire football pitch. The stands are onshore nearby and can seat around 30,000 people.

In Spain, the team Deportivo La Coruna scatters garlic around the pitch to keep away bad spirits. Maybe it worked – from 1991 to 2010 the team was undefeated at home against Real Madrid.

A group of women footballers called Equal Playing Field holds the world record for a match played at the highest altitude. In June 2017, they climbed Mt Kilimanjaro, Tanzania, for six days to reach a volcanic crater at 5,714 metres (18,747 feet) above sea level. There they played the record-setting game to help draw attention to the inequalities women in sport face and to promote sport development for girls and women worldwide.